First U.S. edition 1996

Library of Congress Cataloging-in-Publication Data

Rosen, Michael, 1946–

This is our house / Michael Rosen ; illustrated by Bob Graham.— 1st U.S. ed.

Summary: George won't let any of the other children into his cardboard box house,
but when the tables are turned, he finds out how it feels to be excluded.

ISBN 1-56402-870-4

[1. Selfishness—Fiction.   2. Prejudices—Fiction.   3. Sharing—Fiction.]
I. Graham, Bob, 1942– ill. II. Title.

PZ7.R71867Th   1996
[E]—dc20   95-36137

2 4 6 8 10 9 7 5 3 1

Printed in Hong Kong

This book was typeset in Bob Graham font.
The pictures were done in watercolor, ink, and crayon pencil.

Candlewick Press
2067 Massachusetts Avenue
Cambridge, Massachusetts 02140

This Is
Our House

by
MICHAEL ROSEN

illustrated by
BOB GRAHAM

CANDLEWICK PRESS
CAMBRIDGE, MASSACHUSETTS

George was in the house.

"This house is mine and no one else is coming in," George said.

"It's not your house, George," said Lindy.

"It belongs to everybody."

"No, it doesn't," said George.
"This house is all for me!"

Lindy and Marly went
for a walk over to
the swings.

"It's not George's house,
is it?" said Lindy.
"Of course it isn't," said Marly.

Lindy and Marly looked
in the window.
"It's not your house, George,
and we're coming in."

"Oh, no you're not,"
said George.
"This house isn't for girls."

Freddie was walking past with Rabbity.

"I've come to put Rabbity to bed," said Freddie.

"You can't," said George.

"This house isn't for small people like you."

Freddie took Rabbity for a ride in the car.

Charlene and Marlene fixed the front wheel.

"George won't let me and Rabbity in the house," said Freddie.

Charlene and Marlene, Freddie and Rabbity
headed straight for the house.

"Stop right there," said George.

"We're coming in to fix the fridge,"
said Charlene and Marlene.

"Oh, no you're not," said George.
"This house isn't for twins."

Luther's jumbo jet landed
in the house.
He went to get it.
"Where do you think
you're going?" said George.

"Flight 505 has crashed,"
said Luther, "and I'm
coming in for the rescue.
Fire! Fire! Wee-oo-wee-oo-
wee-oo!"

"You're not coming in here," said George.

Luther radioed for help. "Calling Dr. Sophie. Calling Dr. Sophie."

"Can I help you?" said Sophie.

"We can't get at the plane, Doctor," said Luther.

"Leave it to me," said Sophie.

Sophie and Luther pushed through the crowd.

"Make way for the doctor," said Luther.

"We're coming in," said Sophie.

"Oh, no you're not," said George.
"This house isn't for people
with glasses."

Rasheda had a plan. "I'm going to tunnel in."
She poked her head under the house.
"Go away," said George. "This is my house."
"Well, this is my tunnel," said Rasheda.

"Well, tunnel somewhere else," said
George. "This house isn't for
people who like tunnels."

It was getting very noisy around the house now. And hot.
And George wanted to go to the bathroom.

"I'm going to leave my house now," said George.
"AND NO ONE CAN GO IN IT WHEN I'M GONE."

George went to the bathroom.

Lindy, Marly, Freddie, Rabbity, Marlene, Charlene, Luther, Sophie, and Rasheda went straight into the house.

George came back.

There was no room for George.

"This house isn't for people with red hair," said Charlene.

George started to shout.

George started to cry.

George started to stamp his feet and kick the wall.

Then he stopped.
He looked.

"This house IS for people with red hair," said George,
". . . and for girls and small people and twins, and for
people who wear glasses and like tunnels!"

"Because . . ." shouted Lindy, Marly, Freddie, Marlene, Charlene, Luther, Sophie, and Rasheda,

"THIS HOUSE IS FOR **EVERYONE!**"